EMMie and Mr

Written by Penny Kennedy

and illustrated by Maria Becvar

First published by De Forde Press in 2020

Text and images © Penny Kennedy

ISBN 978-1-5272-6779-4

In memory of Evelyn Kennedy, affectionately known as 'Aunty Effie', on whom the character Emmie is based, and dedicated to my lovely granddaughter, Sophie.

The author would like to thank her husband, Barclay Kennedy, and the rest of her family for all their encouragement; also Dr Kathryn Fleming for her invaluable advice and Derek Rowlinson for typesetting the book. Finally, she would like to express appreciation to Maria Becvar for providing such delightful illustrations.

Emmie was so old that she had long ago forgotten what age she was.

She lived in a very old house that had no gas or electricity and got her water from a well.

An old crooked path led from
the house into a thick forest ...

... and to mountains beyond.

5

In her garden Emmie grew – carrots, potatoes, beans, cabbages, peas ...

... pumpkins, apples, pears, blackberries, raspberries and lots of herbs for medicine.

Nobody came to visit Emmie. People had forgotten she was there. Emmie's friends were her goats, hens, pigs, rabbits, her cat, her dog and her donkey.

9

The donkey helped carry wood from the forest for the fire that heated the house and on which Emmie cooked.

Emmie would wave to people
as they sailed along
the river that flowed
past her house.

She said her prayers every night and was very happy.

"Dear Lord, please watch over me and all my lovely animals as well. Amen."

13

One night, a white rat came through her bedroom window looking for shelter from the rain. Emmie's cat was cross and wanted to chase it. Emmie scolded the grumpy cat and told Mrs Rat that she was welcome to stay.

15

16

But Mrs Rat was very hot and sick. She coughed and coughed and coughed. Emmie tucked her up in a little bed in the corner and gave Mrs Rat a special medicine made of herbs from the garden.

Mrs Rat soon got better thanks to the herbal potion. She had babies in the warm, cosy bedroom. In time, Mrs Rat's babies had their own babies and they all lived together in the shed outside. Emmie was happy to have lots of new friends.

19

One day Emmie realised that
she hadn't seen any boats on
the river for a long, long time.
The birds had all disappeared
too. "What could possibly have
happened?" she wondered.

On a windy day soon after, a newspaper sheet blew into Emmie's garden. She picked it up and read that the whole world was sick – just like Mrs Rat had been.

WORLD NEWS

Emmie decided to try to help. After leaving out lots of food for the animals, she grasped her old blackthorn stick and a bottle of her special medicine.

Then she began a long, hard walk through the forest, over the mountains and into town.

In the town, people wearing masks were standing in their doorways, looking very sick – and astonished. Emmie was astonished too when she turned to see what they were staring at – Mrs Rat and her whole family were trotting along behind!

25

When Emmie and all the rats arrived at the hospital, the doctors and nurses were also amazed at such a sight. Emmie gave the bottle of her special medicine to a doctor and he rushed off to test it on his patients.

After some time, the doctor
returned and exclaimed
excitedly, "Well done, Emmie!
Your medicine is working
already! But we still need to test
a vaccine that will stop people

getting sick again. Perhaps you and your friends could help?" Emmie and Mrs Rat looked at each other and nodded. Of course they could!

Emmie, Mrs Rat and her family all took the vaccine. They were put to bed and tested and checked, tested and checked. Not one of them got a high temperature. Not one of them got the bad cough. Not one of them got sick in any way at all. The vaccine worked!

31

The world would be safe again.

Everyone was so happy and Emmie and all the rats danced with joy!

Everybody wanted to live like Emmie, closer to nature and animals.

35

A statue was made of Emmie and Mrs Rat.

Everyone cheered, "Hooray for Emmie and Mrs Rat!"

Emmie & Mrs Rat

37

THE END

Printed in Germany
by Amazon Distribution
GmbH, Leipzig

21198354R00025